RUMPLEVILLE CHRONICLES

PRESENTS

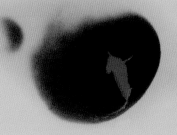

THE
BOMB
THAT
FOLLOWED
ME
HOME

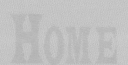

Dedicated to Steven Calhoun

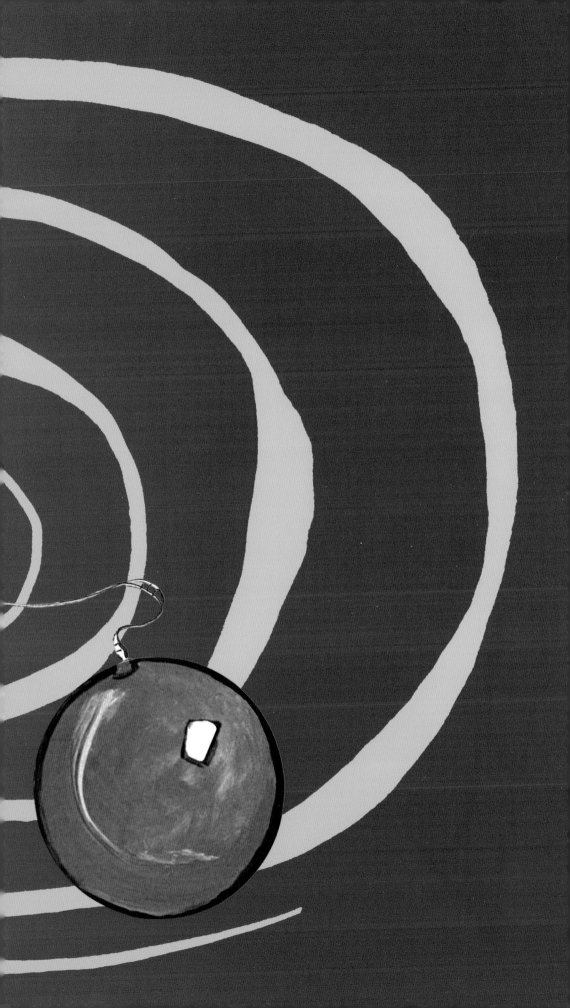

The Bomb That Followed Me Home

Written by
Cevin Soling

Illustrated by
Steve Kille

Designed by
Mark Ohe

Edited/Published by
James M. Crotty

www.rumpleville.com

©2007 Spectacle Films, Inc.
All Rights Reserved

Published by Monk Media
303 Park Avenue South, Suite 1063
NY, NY 10010
www.monkmedia.net

Distributor Orders:
1-800-488-8040

Consumer Orders:
www.rumpleville.com
1-877-TROTSKY

Library of Congress Control Number: 2006928608
ISBN-10: 0-9767771-2-6
ISBN-13: 978-0-9767771-2-0

Printed in China
First Printing, September 2007

One day,
as I was returning home from school,
I noticed a small metal object
lurking in the distance.

It leaped and rolled
behind trees, bushes
and landfills,

whenever I looked back, to avoid being seen. I skipped on, but quickened my pace unsure of whether or not its actions were deliberate.

It tumbled after me,
bowling itself into the yard
behind Mr. Phillips' house, through
the patch of prickle bushes and around
the coniferous trees.

It even
followed me onto
the Greenspans'
lawn, where Mrs.
Greenspan saw me and
began shrieking
incomprehensibly,
as usual.

"Bluagh!!! Urgoakjfa!
Rougaujklb!!!" she
raged. I had no
difficulty translating
her gibberish, as it
was a dialect of
babble I had
learned from
my teachers at school.   It meant,
"Get off my lawn! I am completely
unstable and might burst a blood vessel
 in my brain!!! Bluagh!!!" The word
"bluagh" has no distinct translation,
but probably comes from the
Greek word "blastos,"
meaning "offshoot," which
might imply "off or I'll shoot,"
or possibly that her gibberish wasn't
too good.

I ran as fast as I could to
my house, which seemed
to satisfy Mrs. Greenspan,

although I expected she
would be calling my mother
to complain.

Mrs. Greenspan was a stern old woman who had very little to do with her time except stare at her yard and hope someone would walk across it so she could rail and bellow. The rest of her day was spent

watching game shows and yelling at soap
opera characters for being so stupid. At
night, she would rant at Mr. Greenspan,
whom I often felt sorry for, but not all the
time. He had his moments of crankiness, too.

My parents didn't seem to like the Greenspans much either - at least not since three years ago when the Greenspans planted hedges

several feet into
our property.
My parents
complained to
the Greenspans,
who denied the
charges, so not
much could
be done.

The Greenspans were the type who gave out
carrot sticks and cauliflower on Halloween.
That is, until last year, when they turned
off all their lights and pretended not to be
home so they could stop giving out anything
at all. Mrs. Greenspan hollered at anyone
who ventured up their walk,

"Get off my property! Can't you see the lights are all out? There's nobody home. Now scoot! Bluagh!" She would then phone the police and rant some more. After that, I always wanted to dress up as Mrs. Greenspan for Halloween, but my mom wouldn't let me.

Once I was safely in my yard, I searched around to see what had been behind me, but saw nothing. I ran to my front door and rang the doorbell. As it chimed through my house, I looked back, but whatever had followed me was gone now. Suddenly something chafed against my leg.

I glanced down, and there at my feet was the cutest bomb I had ever seen.

It wagged its fuse and rolled around,
rubbing against my leg. My mother
opened the door and watched the two of
us frolic and gambol.
"Can we keep it?" I pleaded. She shook
her head in gentle disapproval.

"Aw! Why not?"
"Because it's not ours. We have no idea
whom it belongs to.

Why, some crazed anarchist is probably
worried sick wondering where his bomb is!"
"There are no tags or anything. Can't we just
keep it until someone reports it missing?"
"Even if no one claims it, you still can't keep it."
"Why not?" I whined.
"A bomb's a big responsibility," my mom said.
"Who's going to polish it? Who's going to

stand guard over it every night?"
"I will! I will!"
"Oh sure, you say that now, but what about
three months from now? I don't want to be
the one who has to change its fuse every day."
I looked down at its smooth shiny metal.
"I'll take good care of it."
"Well, we'll see what your father says when
he gets home."

The three-and-a-half-hour wait seemed
like eternity. When my father finally
came home, I showed him the bomb,
which I had already named Rusty. It
was going to be that or Kaboom, but I
decided the latter was too fatalistic.

It was final.
Dads are no fun.
They don't like to argue.

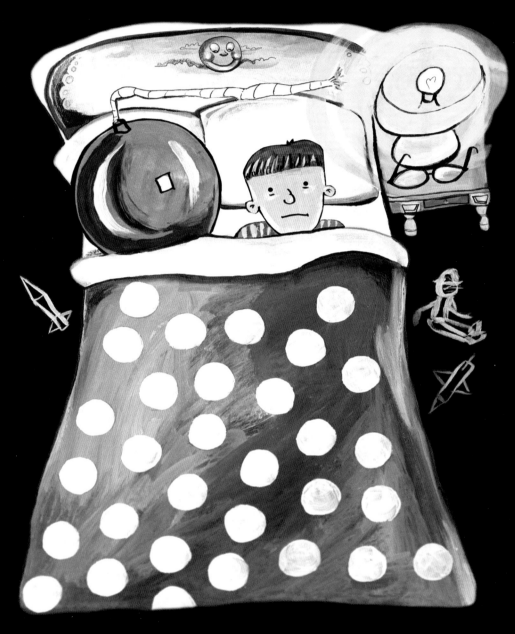

That night I slept with Rusty under my
covers. He seemed to know that it was his
last night with me, and so we sulked together.
The next day Dad made lots of phone calls
to find out where Rusty came from or if
anyone wanted him. He had no luck.

I got to keep Rusty for another day,
but I began to understand a bit more clearly
what my mother had said. Rusty had been
outside all day, and when he rolled back in,
he tracked mud all over the living room
and left powder burns in the den. I had
to wash him and clean up all the mess.

Dad tried the Department of Defense, the National Guard, and even the Weathermen, but couldn't find anyone who wanted to adopt Rusty.

We tried to think of friends
who might have a use for Rusty,
but in the end we all decided
it was best to give him to
the neighbors.

We took
the hedges down
last week.

THE
END

CEVIN SOLING

Cevin Soling's writing career
began when he wrote *The Book Of
Love.* After completing the first murder mystery
written in C++, he invented the only hairbrush endorsed by magicians.

STEVE KILLE

Steve Kille can usually be seen traversing the country playing music with the band
Dead Meadow, making art, or just fueling his stress level with a never-ending need
for espresso.